Trapped

Trapped

Latasha Schaller

Published by Iguana Books
720 Bathurst Street, Suite 303
Toronto, Ontario, Canada
M5S 2R4

Publisher: Kathryn Willms
Editor: Kathryn Willms
Front cover image: Courtesy of iStock
Cover design: Latasha Schaller; Shankari Mano
Book layout design: Shankari Mano

Library and Archives Canada Cataloguing in Publication

Schaller, Latasha, author
Trapped / Latasha Schaller.

Issued in print and electronic formats.
ISBN 978-1-77180-174-4 (hardback).--ISBN 978-1-77180-173-7 (paperback).--ISBN 978-1-77180-175-1 (epub).--ISBN 978-1-77180-176-8 (kindle)

I. Title.

PS8637.C425T73 2016 C813'.6 C2016-902006-1
C2016-902007-X

This is an original print edition of *Trapped*.

The mind is its own place, and in itself
Can make a Heav'n of Hell, a Hell of Heav'n.

—John Milton, *Paradise Lost*

If I leave work now I can make it before the store closes. *If I stay a little longer I won't be able to make it.* If I leave work now I can make it before the store closes. *If I stay just a little longer I won't be able to make it.* I repeat these lines over and over again in my head. I've been repeating them for the past half hour. I will my body to push the chair out so I can stand up, so I can tell Shirley that I'm heading home — that I've done all my work for the day and that I'll see her on Monday. Instead I stay seated and stare at the clock. If I keep waiting I won't make it there in time. I carefully move my stapler back into its place beside the three-hole punch. I make sure my pens, pencils, and highlighters are all in their respective slots within the pencil holder. I shuffle the papers on my desk together, making sure that the edges all line up perfectly. Everything is in its proper place. My first week here a few people in the office thought it would be fun to play a practical joke on me. They moved everything in my office: the books were put out of order; the pictures sitting on my desk were rearranged; even the pens and pencils were thrown haphazardly in the containers on my desk. After they had all gone home I stayed for over an hour putting everything back where it belonged.

Just a little bit longer now.

But despite my internal protests I stop waiting. She's my best friend and it's her favourite store. And it's her birthday. I can suck it up and do this; I can go in there and get the sweater that Emily's been admiring for the past month. She dragged me into the store last week just to show it to me, to make me see the "most amazing sweater," the one she needs in her life but can't buy because then she wouldn't be able to afford groceries for a week. She's my best friend. If she can help me deal with all my crap I can do this one small thing for her. I can do this. I will do this.

I stand up, push in my chair, and make my way down the hall.

I gently knock on Shirley's door, hoping that she doesn't have any clients in. The last time, I accidentally interrupted an impromptu meeting with an author whose last novel had brought in a quarter of a million dollars within the first month of publication, and whose next project was underway. Needless to say I got reamed out afterwards and went home crying, convinced that I was going to lose my job; a job I'd only had for three weeks by that point. Since then I've done my best to stay on Shirley's good side. I make sure to always come in early and to stay late at least twice a week; I always offer to help out when there's an opportunity, and there are plenty of opportunities when you're the newest employee of a multi-billion-dollar publishing house. I ease open the door. Luckily for me Shirley is not in a meeting, and judging by the smile on her face I've caught her in an unexpectedly good mood.

Despite her elevated position in the company Shirley's quite young; if I had to guess her age I'd say mid-thirties. I'm not much younger than her, but I doubt that I will be able to move up the ladder fast enough to be at the same level by the time I'm her age. It's something to aspire to. Around the office we speculate how much she actually makes — because who doesn't wonder how much more money their boss "earns" — but we really have no idea. The general consensus is that it's at least six figures, but that still leaves a huge range of possibilities. Judging by her appearance, though, and the pictures of her house and wedding in her office, she's doing well. I've been here for about six weeks, and I haven't seen her wear the same outfit twice. She has blazers and pantsuits and dress skirts in just about every shade of blue, grey, and black that you can imagine, and these aren't off-the-rack clothes from the Eaton Centre. I'm talking completely tailored pieces that probably cost more than Patrick and my groceries for a month. I'd be lying if I said I didn't want her entire wardrobe, accessories included.

"Hi, Charlie, I was actually on my way to go talk to you. Please sit." She motions towards the bright red chair in front of her desk. She barely waits for me to be seated before she begins speaking, punctuating her words with gestures as if she's conducting a symphony only she can see. "I spoke with Ryan at the beginning of the week: I wanted to see how the transition between editors had gone for him, and of course how his latest novel is coming along. As I'm sure you've come to realize, Ryan has a different way of looking at things; he's one of our more ... subversive ... authors. After Candace left I didn't think we'd find the right person for him. But he said that you've helped a lot and provided some new ways to attack different parts of his story, which he's extremely grateful for. He especially stressed the value of your insights into the main character's motivation behind the killing of his daughter; all of which I'm very happy to hear. Because when our clients are happy, I'm happy." She pauses here, as if to let the importance of her happiness and what it means for me sink in.

"I know that when you were hired you were told it's company policy to wait until after the three-month grace period to allow you to take on any more authors, but after my conversation with Ryan and the work I've seen you do around the office I've decided to waive this. I spoke with my bosses, and we've agreed to let you start reading manuscripts. We have a substantial base of bestselling authors — we're hoping that you can help us find more. I think you have a unique perspective that can benefit this company. And yourself."

Oh my god. Oh my god oh my god oh my god! This is incredible. This is amazing.

This is definitely not the right time to ask if I can get out of work early. Shit. *At least now I won't have to worry about Free People.* But what about Emily's present?

"Wow, thank you. I've also enjoyed working with Ryan, and I truly appreciate the opportunity you're giving me. I promise that I will do my best to find projects that I believe in and that I think will be a success."

"I would expect nothing less. Monday morning you'll meet with Sarah and she'll go over what you'll be doing and what we look for in a potential author and manuscript." Shirley turns towards her computer and it's obvious that our conversation is done — it's the longest conversation I've had with her since my interview. I say thank you again and she nods her head in acknowledgement, her mind already preoccupied with the latest author email.

"Oh, and Charlie—" I turn back towards her, my hand already grasping the doorknob, "why don't you go home early. Enjoy your last calm weekend before the craziness begins." She smiles, briefly, but her eyes narrow as she turns back towards her computer screen and I know it's time to get the hell out of there.

"Will do, thanks." I quietly shut the door and half-walk half-run back to my office. I can't believe what just happened. I snap back to reality when I get to my office and see the time on my computer screen. 4:30. I have an hour and a half until the store closes. *Shit shit shit.* I can make it there after all.

@ @ @

A short ten-minute subway ride later I find myself standing in front of the store looking up at its sign: Free People. I should've come at a different time — it's too busy now; people pour in and out, people who clearly frequent the store. *People who belong in the store and in the clothes. People who aren't me. I can't go in there. I can't. I don't belong in that store — they're all going to know it as soon as they look at me. The employees will follow me around offering to help, and the other customers will take one look at my outfit and know that I shouldn't be in there.* I'm overreacting, I'm fine. It'll only take a few minutes. I know exactly where the sweaters are, so I will just grab one and head straight to pay. *But what if they moved the sweaters? What if I have to blindly walk around looking for them? They'll know that I have no idea what I'm doing. I'll look like such an idiot.* I nervously look around me, watching the people mill about. *I wonder how many people are talking about me. I'm sure that woman on the bench beside me is talking about me with her friend. And I swear I saw a group of teenage girls pointing and staring at me. They all know. Great idea, Charlie. Just look at all the people looking at you.* I snap my head down and focus on my nails: picking and pulling at the loose skin around them, trying to improve their look.

But this is for Emily. I can go in there and buy the sweater. I'm making too big a deal of this. It's just a store. I go into stores all the time. *But I'm too out of place here — I don't fit in. I don't match the boho-hippie vibe the place gives off. I'm wearing dress pants for fuck's sake.* Come on, Charlie, don't be like this. I need to stop spiralling. It's just a store. It's just a sweater. It's the perfect birthday present and I know Emily will love it. *But I can't. I can't do this.* I look back up at the sign, but this time I can barely make out the words. I wipe away the tears that I've unknowingly let escape. To the outside world I look like some weirdo, some freak who stands outside stores for minutes on end just staring. Would they think I was any less weird if they could see what was going on in my head? If they could hear the argument with myself, or my unsuccessful attempts to calm myself down? *Probably not; they'd think I'm crazy.*

I can do this, I can do this.

I finally take a step towards the door, then another, my eyes locked on the sign. I freeze. *I can't go in there like this — I'm visibly upset. They'll think I'm a huge weirdo. Who cries walking into a store? No, I shouldn't go in. I can't go in.*

"What the fuck is her problem?" *Who said that?* I look around to see the speaker but stop when we make eye contact. She's looking over her shoulder at me: the idiot who didn't move out of the way to let her and her boyfriend pass as they left the store. Completely oblivious. I begin to back away from the store, bumping into more people as I do. *I am such a loser. How did I not see them? They must think I'm so fucking weird. I am weird. I'm standing outside this store talking to myself, trying to work up the nerve to go in. This is fan-fucking-tastic. I can't do this. What was I thinking even coming here? I'm sure the people inside have been watching me idiotically standing here. They probably saw what just happened: oh god, they're probably talking about me now. They'll go home and tell all their friends about it. I can't go in there. I bet they're all just laughing at me, like that couple is.*

I pull out my phone; it's 5:20. The store closes in forty minutes.

Standing outside looking in is completely pointless and useless. I'm not going in and I'm just wasting time. I stare at the blank phone screen, racking my brain for some solution. I need to get that sweater; we're going out for supper to celebrate her birthday tomorrow...

I dial the first number that comes to mind and try to calm my quivering voice.

"Hey, Patrick, I don't have much time to talk — yeah, I'm swamped at work. I don't think I'll be able to grab Emily's birthday present on my way home.

"I know, I know. I should've gone sooner and not waited till the last minute. But can you please just do this? I promise to make it worth your while... No. No. Fine. Deal.

"I'll send you the info so they can help you at the store. Yeah, I'll make sure to send a picture from their website and the size and whatnot.

"It's Free People. Do you know where that is?

"Awesome, thank you! You're the best." Relieved I turn away from the store and head back towards the subway station, past the hordes of people clamouring to spend their hard-earned money in the overpriced stores that line the street. Oh Toronto: narcissism capital of Canada.

It's not until I get off at my stop that I realize I need to kill some time — I can't beat Patrick home because then he'll know that something's up. There's not much between the stop and our house, save a few take-out places and a ridiculously overpriced laundromat. I decide to stop in at Shoppers; I have a sudden craving for something sweet.

@ @ @

When I get home Patrick's, thankfully, already there and the house smells delicious. I place my keys on the rack beside the large mirror in the entryway, and check for any evidence of tears. Unlike many people on the subway I hate checking my face in public spaces; it feels like everyone is watching. But I allowed myself a quick check on my ride home, and now, looking in the mirror, I can see what I missed: there are still lines in my blush where the tears ran down my face, and there's residual mascara underneath my chin. I really need to remember to pick up some waterproof mascara, especially with summer fast-approaching in this disgustingly humid city. I don't even want to think about what the heat is going to do to my hair.

Making my way into the house I'm happy to see two pizza boxes from our favourite pizza place, sitting on the kitchen island beside a bag bearing the name "Free People." What would I do without him? I reach out to grab the bag, to make sure Patrick got the right sweater, but before I can grasp it he places a glass of white wine in my hand. He's all smiles.

"Sounds like you were having a busy day at work so I thought it'd be nice for you to come home to some wine and pizza." His smile gets even bigger, travelling up to his eyes and lighting his face up. While he pours himself a glass of wine I grab us plates from the cabinet behind me, relieved that we've finally bought a full set of dishes and are no longer using the random pieces that our parents gave us when we each moved out. Free dishes are nice but having a complete set of matching white dinner plates, instead of a mix of plastic dishes and cups, makes me feel like an actual adult. Admittedly, though, we kept a few cups with our plastic containers in the kitchen because Patrick argued that you never know when they might come in handy.

"Figured I'd give you the night off cooking duty." As he says this I almost snort out my wine: after only a few bites of pizza he has managed to spill tomato sauce down his shirt and get some on his nose. I swear sometimes he eats like a toddler. I can't even count the white shirts he's gone through — they're like a magnet for spills. On our wedding day I made him tuck a napkin into his collar so that he wouldn't get stains all over his suit. He still brings it up when we look at wedding photos; many of which have since surfaced document his embarrassment. I gently remind him that because of what I did his clothes remained spotless and we were able to get many nice pictures of us afterwards; that is until he and his groomsmen decided it would be hilarious to take their ties off and wear them around their heads because apparently they're sixteen. But I digress.

With my free hand I grab the Free People bag. "Thanks for getting this for me. I really appreciate it. Plus I know Emily will love it, so thank you from her too. Can you pull it out so I can make sure it's the right one? My hands are a little full."

"If you insist," Patrick says as he sets the bag on one of the island's chairs and begins to take off his dress pants. Such a comedian, this one. After the day I've had I'm tempted to let him keep going — it would be a great distraction — but I need to make sure he got the right sweater; I'd feel horrible if it wasn't the right one, and it would be all my fault. *It would be Patrick's; I even sent him a picture of it.* Nice try, but Patrick wouldn't be the one to blame. I honestly don't even think I'd tell him because he would feel bad and then I would feel bad for making him feel bad because it's my own fault. Gah.

I finish the slice in my hand, making sure to wipe the grease off on one of the napkins Patrick laid out, and pick the bag up from the chair handing it to him once again.

"I'd rather see the sweater."

With a huff he says, "Fine," and slowly pulls the pants up from around his ankles and does them up. He grumbles under his breath and the only thing I catch is "piece of meat" as he pulls the sweater from the bag. As he unfolds it I hear something hit the hardwood, but he snatches it up before I can get to it.

"And what's that?" I ask, pointing to whatever it is he stuffed back into the bag.

"Just a little something I saw at the store that I thought you'd like. I'm surprised you don't go there; there's some really nice stuff. Think I might go back for your birthday next month."

He holds the sweater up.

"But did I get the right one? I got a gift receipt in case I didn't — or if it's the wrong size or whatever." He genuinely looks concerned so there is an audible sigh of relief when I tell him that it is. After I check the size and make sure everything's right we head into the living room to enjoy the rest of the wine and pizza. I grab a handful of extra napkins; it's only a matter of time until Patrick drops a pepperoni on himself or I spill my wine. We make quite the pair. Once we're all settled and cozy with some big blankets and one of our favourite shows, he tells me to close my eyes and open my hands. I'm half-tempted to make a dirty joke but restrain myself and do as he says, excited to find out what he got me. I feel him place something cool into my hand.

"Okay, you can open your eyes." I do as soon as the words leave his mouth and see a silver cuff sitting in my palm: it looks like several overlapping coins with various symbols and designs stamped into them in a cyclical pattern. Their shape and size remind me of the ancient drachmas we saw in the Delphi Archaeological Museum. "When I saw this it reminded me of our honeymoon, and I know you own a few bracelets like this, so I thought you would like it." It's beautiful.

"I love it." I put the bracelet on and admire it from all angles, knowing how happy my reaction is making Patrick. "I'll wear it to work on Monday; I have the perfect outfit for it."

"Great." He smiles and pulls me in for a hug. "How was your day, though? Is it getting busier? Are they getting you to do more stuff around the office?"

I've been so focused on the sweater I've completely forgotten to share my fantastic news; I spend the next half hour telling Patrick about my talk with Shirley and what it means for me and my position. By the end he's grinning from ear to ear.

"Wow, Charlie! That's incredible, I'm so happy for you. I've been worried about how much you like your job here and everything – and that you might resent moving here because of me, because of my job." He pauses to collect his thoughts, refusing to look me in the eye. "It was a big move from Winnipeg, and I know Toronto wasn't exactly your dream place to live. But it makes me feel better knowing that you're doing well at work."

"How many times do I have to tell you I didn't move here for you; I moved here for us. We knew I would find work and your job brings in more money — this just makes sense. And look at how well you're doing at work; didn't you just say that Morgan wants to bring you in on the McLean case? I'm so proud of you and I will always support you and whatever decision is best for your career."

I meet his eyes and smile. "But thanks ... for worrying; it lets me know that you actually think about what the move has been like for me." I know that Patrick wants to say something about this, so I quickly change the subject. "I love my job though, and I'm still kind of in shock from my talk with Shirley. It's insane. I've only been there for a month and a half!" I feel as if I'm glowing with happiness. In all honesty I never dreamed I would love my job as much as I do. Especially after the anxiety I felt about moving to a new city; I'm surprised I didn't drive Patrick crazy with my incessant checking of everything we had packed and everything we planned on leaving behind.

"That's my girl!" He clinks his wine glass against mine and gives a toast to my future successes. "Dessert?" I ask. "I stopped off and grabbed us some chocolate bars on the way home. Can you grab my purse from the kitchen? They're in there."

"Nice! Where from?" Patrick asks as he gets up and retrieves the purse: a birthday present from him last year that he bought on our trip to New York, and my constant go-to. There's just something classic about black and gold.

"Just Shoppers. I had a craving." Patrick passes me my purse as he sits back down on the couch. I reach inside and pull out a small white bag, and hand it to Patrick. "I got one package of Reese's Peanut Butter Cups and a Kit Kat, so grab whichever." A look of shock spreads over his face as he looks in the bag; his eyes widen and his hands begin to shake. He looks from the bag to me, and then back from me to the bag. And instead of a chocolate bar Patrick pulls out my other purchase from Shoppers. The one I'd completely forgotten about.

"Are you? Is this? Have you taken one yet? I didn't even know you were late... Why didn't you say anything?" His speech gets faster with each question. He picks up his glass of wine from the coffee table, slams it down, and then refills it as fast as he can reach the bottle — all while clutching the pregnancy test in his other hand. The sun's begun to set and neither of us has turned the living room lights on yet, so we sit in TV-lit darkness.

"Careful, don't break it," I say. His hand is clenched so tightly around the box that the flimsy cardboard is on the verge of being reduced to a crumpled ball despite the fact that there's a plastic stick in there that I need to pee on. I'll be surprised if he didn't mangle the stick too with how forcefully he closed and tightened his hand.

"Shit, sorry." He immediately opens his hand and lets the box fall onto his lap. We both stare at it in silence. I can hear his breathing quickening and try to say something to calm him down.

"I'm only a few days late, which isn't much, but I'm usually on time so I figured I'd just pick one up to check and be safe. I'm sure everything's fine, I just wanted to make sure." I put down my fourth glass of wine and pick up the box from Patrick's lap. "After all that wine I have to pee so might as well do it now." He looks like he's going to puke, but he gets up and follows me upstairs to our ensuite. He starts to come into the bathroom with me but backs out when he remembers that I have to pee on a stick.

"I'll, uh, just be out here." He drags a hand up his face and through his hair. He's still holding the bottle of wine in the other. "I'm going to change into some sweats." He grabs mine too and tosses them at me before the bathroom door can shut. I look at myself in the mirror, staring into my eyes as I tell myself that everything is going to be okay. Just breathe. I sit down on the toilet and read over the instructions; I know you're supposed to pee on the thing and it's pretty foolproof, but it's my first time doing one and I don't want to fuck it up. While I do the test, I can hear Patrick outside pacing back and forth waiting for me and the results. If I take any longer there will be a path worn in the hardwood given how hard and fast he's walking. As soon as I've flushed the toilet and start washing my hands Patrick has opened the door and come inside. He reaches for the stick then hesitates, probably because he has no idea which part I peed on.

"So what does it say?" Even though he tries to keep his voice calm, his face betrays his anxiety. He stares at me with worried eyes as I pick up the test to read the results. He sits down on the toilet seat, and judging from the way he looks, it's probably a good idea: closer to the ground if he faints. I stare down at the pregnancy test in my hands, the small piece of plastic that has the potential to completely change the rest of our lives forever, and I read what it says. I look up at Patrick. Our eyes meet.

"I'm pregnant." I'm pregnant. I'm pregnant. I am pregnant. I'm going to have a baby.

"Well, okay." He looks down at his watch and gets up. Walking past me he stops to give me a hug and to say that he has to go. Apparently he's meeting some of the guys from work to celebrate the case they just won. He apologizes for the bad timing, changes into a pair of jeans, and leaves the room. I want to move, to follow him through our room and down the stairs, but I can't. I'm frozen. The entire house is silent save for the opening and closing of the front door which, by the sound of it, was done as gently as possible. I look at the pregnancy test in my hand, the little symbol declaring my pregnancy staring back at me, and I wonder what the hell to do now.

"What the hell just happened?" I ask into the silence.

Nothing good.

@ @ @

At 4 a.m. I'm instantly awoken when Patrick slams the front door and staggers up the stairs. As if his entrance hadn't made enough noise he flings open the bedroom door as hard as he can and smacks the light switch until it turns on. His t-shirt is covered in god-knows-what, and I can smell him before he's fully entered the room – the stench makes my stomach turn. Whiskey. He begins emptying his pockets, throwing his wallet, keys, and loose change onto the floor for me to pick up tomorrow; he seems happy about the amount of money still left in his wallet and fist pumps the air. He grins sheepishly when he notices me staring.

"Ah, there she is, my beau-u-u-utiful wife." Patrick falls to the floor before he can even get the words out and begins taking his clothes off right there, leaning backwards as he struggles with his pants. Clothes become intermingled with the contents of his pockets, and he whimpers as he accidentally stabs himself with his keys when he tries to pull his legs free from the jeans. I try hard to suppress a laugh because encouragement is the last thing he needs right now. He manages to get trapped in his shirt for a few minutes. I don't even know how, but at one point he has both arms going through the neck hole. He's some kind of special. When he's finished, and sitting completely naked on the floor, I finally speak.

"Do you have any idea what time it is? I haven't heard from you all night, Patrick, and you smell like you bathed in whiskey." He tries to point his finger at me, but his entire body is swaying and his eyes can't focus whatsoever; he might be trying to point at three of me for all I know, which would explain the wide space around me that Patrick includes in the attempt.

"Nuh uh, smarty-pants. It's—" he hiccups and pauses to make sure nothing's coming up, "rum. Rum rum rum." Patrick crawls across the room to the bed and tries to pull himself up onto his side; he fails miserably and I'm forced to help him up. I'm tempted to let him sleep on the floor, but I don't feel like hearing him complain tomorrow about how hungover and sore he is. Not that he doesn't deserve both.

After he had left, and I was finally out of the shocked state that he left me in, I had called him. No answer. I'd left three voicemails and texted him several times. Nothing. Frustrated, I'd spent the rest of the evening completely cleaning the main floor: filling and emptying the dishwasher, folding and putting away our blankets, wrapping up the leftover pizza, and throwing the boxes into recycling. I had started putting our clothes away but given up after I'd broken several hangers in anger. Before I fell asleep I had texted a few guys he works with, telling them to give me a call or text if they needed me to come pick him up. Not a single one did.

Once I get him under the covers I head downstairs and grab a glass of water for him. I'm wide awake now so I might as well be useful, and I'd rather get the water myself than have him stumble down the stairs in an hour when he wakes up thirsty and incoherent. He's not the most graceful of people when sober, and this is the first time he's come home this drunk by himself. We usually have each other to lean on coming up the stairs. Or to drag. Or carry. Although the one time I tried to carry him up the stairs, I almost dropped him head first and had to abandon that plan in a hurry.

When I get back to Patrick he's mumbling something under his breath about rum rhyming with bum, and he's completely unaware of my presence until I hand him the water and tell him to drink up.

"Oh I have — I have! So many drinks. All of the drinks." He smiles to himself as if remembering something from earlier on in the evening, but then stops and tries to push himself up off the bed. It takes him a few minutes to place his cup on the bedside table; he's swaying so much. Thank god I got him a plastic one; I do not feel like taking care of another mess tonight. I push down on his chest to stop him from getting up, and he tries to push my hands away but ends up hitting himself in the face. "And what do you think you're doing, missy?" He shoves his face into mine and I have to hold my breath; his is so strong.

"Stopping you from getting up. I got you into bed once; I'm not doing it a second time." He starts giggling when I say "into bed," but I talk over him, trying to get him to listen to me. "If you need anything just tell me and I'll grab it." He folds his arms across his chest, giving me the best angry look he can with one eye partially closed and his head still slowly swaying from side to side.

"Stop telling me what to do. First you tell me I'm having a kid, and now that I can't even stand up?" If he tried to stand up he would fall flat on his face. Or his ass. But apparently I'm the bad guy for trying to stop that from happening. "Who do you think you are? Hmmmmm?" Before I can respond his closed eye shoots open and he brings both hands to his mouth; I barely have enough time to run into the bathroom and grab the bucket from underneath the sink before the vomit escapes him. I try to rub his back as he heaves into the container, but he shakes his head and spits out, "I'm fine" in between bursts of puking. I'm forced to just sit there waiting for him to be done, and when he is I take the bucket from him and clean it out, making sure to place it on the floor on his side of the bed in case he needs it again. I damn near puke myself while cleaning it; I think I'll be forever haunted by that partially digested cheese-rum mixture.

"Patrick ... I just found out I'm pregnant; was I supposed to lie and say that I wasn't? Besides, being pregnant and having a kid are not necessarily the same thing." I know it makes absolutely no sense to talk to him right now, but I can't help it. *I need to talk to him — he didn't let me before, and I need to hear what he has to say. Regardless of what he's done — especially because of what he's done.* This is a bad idea; he's absolutely shit-faced right now. It's not fair to get into this when he's in this state. *Fuck fair. Was it fair for him to just get up and leave me all alone after finding out that I'm pregnant? Is it fair that he came home at 4 a.m. and woke me up? Is it fair that I have to take care of his drunken ass?*

"Yeah, it is the same thing." His eye remains open; maybe throwing up helped. "You said you're pregnant, which means we're having a kid."

"But the way you say it sounds so negative, like you don't have a choice."

"I do?" For a moment the drunkenness seems to fade away, and a look of pure astonishment and realization flits across his face. He does?

"Of course." *What am I doing? What am I saying?* This can't end well.

"Then I don't." He uncrosses his arms and slides down under the covers, pulling them over his head.

"You don't what, Patrick?" No. No. No. No. I scream the word over and over again in my mind, trying to drown out the memory of what he just said. He peeks his head out and looks at me, and I can no longer tell how drunk or sober he is. His face is completely blank.

"I don't want to have a kid." He passes out before he can say another word, before he can hear the catch in my throat as I try to stop the tears from falling. I slowly get up off the bed. I look down at the pile of stuff on the floor, and as much as I want to leave it for him to clean I pick everything up, put it all away, and turn the lights off.

What am I supposed to do? Is he going to leave me if I have it? Is he going to try to talk me out of having it? Is he going to change his mind? Did he really mean that?

I spend the next hour lying in bed awake, my mind spiralling out of control. One idea turns into another and that turns into another until I've completely lost what holds the threads of thought together. At first I try to quiet my mind, to calm myself and my thoughts, but I can't. All day I cling to the tenuous grasp I have on my ability to think rationally, but in the darkness of night I can no longer hold on. The line between rational and irrational thought is completely obliterated, and I can no longer differentiate between the voice of anxiety and the voice of reason. Lying in the dark I'm overrun with the fears and doubts that hide in the shadows during the day. I try to fight against them; to remind myself that they're problems and thoughts my own mind has created. And that I can stop them. But I can't. The anxious voice within my mind is too strong, its opposition too weak. By the end the two are so blurred together that I can no longer tell them apart. I can no longer tell which voice is winning. Or which has already won.

@ @ @

The next morning I come downstairs to a very haggard and hungover-looking husband; Patrick's sitting at the island with his head cradled in his hands and a giant bottle of purple Gatorade beside him. The blinds are closed and he's sitting in complete darkness; he flinches when I open the fridge and the light hits him. Wow. Apparently he remembers nothing of coming home the night before: not puking or needing help into bed or talking. Nothing. He apologizes several times, for his behaviour after finding out I'm pregnant and for his bad timing in leaving. He claims the latter was unavoidable. How true that is, I don't know, but I don't feel like arguing so I leave it. Instead I bring up the pregnancy again, and his face becomes still. He's quiet for a few minutes, and when he begins to speak it's softly.

"I mean in all honesty I'm completely freaking the fuck out right now, mostly because you seem so calm about all of this. I just wasn't expecting this." He points to my stomach when he says "this," but quickly pulls his hand away when he realizes what he's doing and how it comes across. Both hands resume their position on either side of his head. He closes his eyes again, but I start talking.

"Neither of us did. I'm freaking out too. This is a huge life-changing thing, and it's extremely terrifying and serious, but it's kind of exciting at the same time."

"It is. It's just..." He trails off. My heart sinks.

"It's just?" And despite everything that's happened I can't help but hope that he might surprise me and this might take a positive turn.

"I just don't think this is the right time for us. We just moved here a few months ago, and we're still getting this place set up. Our bedroom still needs to be painted, unless you've grown to love that horrible yellow wallpaper, and the basement is completely unfinished. I mean, luckily the main floor is pretty much done, but it's not even fully furnished yet; we only have two chairs for the dining room set.

"Add onto that the fact that your work is giving you this huge opportunity and that you will have been there for less than a year before you go on maternity leave... I just think that we need to take some time and really think about this." He finishes talking, and I'm stunned into silence for a solid five minutes; the longer I'm quiet the more worried he becomes. "Charlie, come on. I just..." But I cut him off.

"You what? Patrick ... there is no ideal time to have children. There just isn't. We're never going to be fully happy with the house or with our jobs; it's the human condition to want more than you have.

"But at the same time," and with this, I raise up my clenched fists and forcefully release them, "what the fuck. Could you not just let things settle for, like, I don't know — a day — before you completely tore my heart out? I think I want this baby, Patrick. And yeah, you're right, the timing isn't ideal, but we'll figure it out. And if you won't I will." I get up off the stool beside him and leave the room because I can't bear to look at him right now. He tries to grab my hand and make me stay. He pleads with me, saying that he wants to talk and that he's sorry if he came across too harsh; he was just trying to be honest. But I just can't. I can't listen to him right now. I've never walked out during an argument before because I've always hated the idea of it; I feel like it's a childish and unnecessary thing to do, but now I feel like I have no other choice. I grab my keys and purse and make my way to the front door. Before I can slam it shut I hear Patrick say quietly, "I'm sorry, Charlie, I really am." And so am I.

@ @ @

"He said WHAT?!" I swear half of Starbucks turns around; Emily is full-out yelling. She slams both hands on the table, and I have to grab my iced coffee before it flies off the table from the shock of the impact. This isn't an unusual occurrence, though; Emily is easily the loudest and most outspoken person that I know, and it isn't uncommon for her to be asked to quiet down at restaurants, movie theatres, and even museums. I just hope she doesn't notice the people staring at her because after what I've just told her I don't want her going off on someone. She also has a terrible temper and the shortest fuse imaginable. She met her current boyfriend at a Starbucks; he went to grab her drink, thinking it was his, and she actually smacked his hand out of the way. Long story short we've since learnt that he's not opposed to getting a light smack now and again.

"I know... I didn't know whether to scream at him, slap him, or sucker-punch him right in the face. I get that he was scared and it freaked him out, I really do, but my god; did he really think THAT was the right thing to say at the time? I'm all for honesty, but I mean..." I sip my drink, watching the bracelet Patrick gave me slide up and down my wrist. As mad as I am at him I do really love the bracelet, and I couldn't wait to wear it today. He looked so full of hope when I put it on this morning, but when he complimented me on how well it went with my outfit, all I gave him was a terse thanks and a reminder of when I'd be home after work. I was seriously tempted to purposely not wear the bracelet, but I decided that would be too mean. While a small part of me desperately wants to hurt him the way that he hurt me, I can't.

Em plays with her straw wrapper as she considers the situation, folding it smaller and smaller until she can't physically make it bend any further. "Oh, it's absolute bullshit. Look, I'm not saying he didn't make some valid points," she stops when she feels my glare but disregards it and keeps going, "you have to admit that he did. You guys haven't been here for long and now with this change at work – which I'm still super excited for you about, yay!" She makes a fist and pumps the air. "It's just a lot of new stuff to deal with at once. I'm not saying the guy's right, and he definitely should've waited to say anything, but I don't think he's fully wrong either."

Goddammit. I fold my arms onto the small table and drop my head onto them.

I can't help but sigh. She's right, and we both know it.

When I look back up, Em's face has softened, a rare thing to see. "I know. It's just ... why did that have to be his first response, you know? I get it if we were having a conversation a week or two later, once we'd wrapped our minds around it all, and he'd said that ... but for that to be the first thing he had to say? It just felt absolutely horrible; it still does." Emily nods her head in agreement, and my eyes can't help but wander around the room looking at all the mothers with their kids: babies, toddlers, teenagers. It makes me happy because I'm going to finally be one of them, or at least I'm on my way. "It just sucks. I wish he was happier about it, I really do. Because I want this," I hold my hands against my non-existent belly, feeling where the little life inside of me is growing, "but I don't know what I'm supposed to do if he doesn't. What do I do?" I quickly move my hands off my stomach and to my face, embarrassed to be crying in the middle of Starbucks on a Monday afternoon. Emily pushes the remaining half of her brownie across the table to me.

"Chocolate helps." I give her a small smile in return for hers. And for the chocolate.

"I must really be screwed if you're willing to give up half a brownie." I devour the chocolate in a few quick bites, but it doesn't stop the gnawing feeling in my stomach.

"You're not screwed ... it's just not the most ideal of situations." She pulls a baggie of Oreos from her purse and hands them to me; the girl eats every unhealthy thing imaginable, and a lot of it, yet somehow manages to stay a tiny little thing. Once she told me that in high school she actually went on a "hunger strike" at home because her mom refused to buy her Double Stuf Oreos, and won. Right now I'm grateful for her terrible eating habits because there is nothing I want more when I'm sad than sugary foods — something Em knows well. "Have you guys talked about it at all since you found out?" She snatches a cookie out of the baggie between us and pops the whole thing into her mouth.

"Nope. We've barely talked... He keeps trying to talk to me, but I just can't. I can't forget what he said, and every time he goes to open his mouth that's all I can think about. And it breaks my heart because I can see how horrible he feels about it. I even heard him crying yesterday when I came home from the market." Just thinking about it makes the tears well up in my eyes.

"I'm scared that talking to him about it will only make things worse. What if he tells me he doesn't want the baby? Am I supposed to choose between the two? How am I supposed to do that?" The crying has slowly started to build, and I have to stop talking in order to hold back the force of my tears. Emily scoots her chair all the way around the table till she's sitting beside me; she wraps her arms around me and tries to get me to calm down. But I can't. I can't. *Because what if this isn't what he wants? What if he tells me again that he doesn't want this baby — our baby? What am I supposed to do?* I can't help but think back to all the times I've watched him play with his nieces: how they cling to him when we leave and how much he enjoys spoiling them. And it hurts. It hurts so goddamn much.

The alarm on my phone goes off, and I'm jolted back to reality. "Fuck, I have to get back to work." I detangle myself from Emily and gather up my stuff, making sure to swipe the bag with the few remaining cookies inside.

"Sorry that I took over the conversation entirely, I know you're stressed about meeting Eric's parents for the first time. I'll see you later at spin though, and we can talk about it then?"

She lightly smacks my arm. "Don't apologize; you should've told me sooner."

"But Saturday was your birthday..." Em rolls her eyes as I say this.

"Screw my birthday, this is more important." She ignores me when I shake my head "no." "But, shit, I forgot to tell you; I can't make it to the gym. His parents get in this afternoon and we're going out for supper tonight. Rain check?"

Fuck. "Yeah, no problem." We walk together outside, the sun blinding us both. "Give me a call once they're gone, or during the visit if they're making you too crazy, and we'll make plans to get together. Thanks for this, though; normally I'd talk to Patrick when something makes me this upset, but..." There are just some things I can't tell him.

"It's what I'm here for. I'll talk to you later — assuming I survive tonight. Bye!"

I watch Emily walk to her car then turn and speed walk to the subway station; if I'm late Sarah will be pissed and Shirley will kill me. Luckily, and thanks to my half-running from my stop to the office, I make it back with five minutes to spare. The few extra minutes are just what I need to fix my hair and makeup — removing all traces of crying.

@ @ @

I walk into the spin room and encounter row upon row of toned, terrifying women. Everyone seems to be talking at once and attempting to talk over the woman behind her, beside her, and in front of her. Because I'm later than normal almost all of the spots are taken. The only free bikes are in the front row, which is of course the worst spot in the entire room. Not only can everyone behind you see you, but the instructor gives the front the hardest time. That's fine, though; I'm already here so I might as well just go sit down. Besides, after all those cookies today I could use a good ass-kicking. But I don't budge. *This is only my third time coming. I still have no idea what I'm doing, and I'll look like a complete fool if I sit in the front.* Well, where the hell else am I supposed to go? I can't exactly bring one of those bikes to the back — talk about drawing attention to myself. *Yes, I should keep arguing with myself while I stand in the doorway looking like a complete buffoon.* Then I should just go sit down; solves everything. *Does not. I can't sit at the front. Look at the four girls already sitting up there! I look nothing like them: with their head-to-toe Lululemon and their perfect ponytails just bouncing along.* They look more like they're ready to go to a photoshoot than work out — I look more ready for this class. *Yeah, with my hair all piled on top of my head and wearing workout clothes I bought at Walmart — I'm the model of what a woman should look like at the gym.* At least I'm not wearing makeup like they are; that just makes them look stupid.

I don't want to go in there alone. I've never had to go by myself; Em's always come with me before. Well, she can't tonight; I knew that and still came. I knew I'd be working out by myself when I got here. Yeah, but I also spent the entire subway ride here working up the nerve to come inside the gym. And before that I spent all afternoon agonizing over whether I would get on the subway to come here or on the one to go home. I need to decide; the class is about to start, and now there's only one spot left and I'm still standing in the doorway.

"Hi, I've seen you here before. Are you coming in?" Shit. I look to my right and standing beside me is the class instructor; she's even more beautiful up close and easily has the best body I've ever seen in real life. She makes the girls sitting at the front look like cheap knock offs. I wish I looked like her.

"Um..." She smiles expectantly, waiting for me to get my head out of the clouds and to bounce into the class with her. I need to give her an answer. Anything. The entire class has now turned their heads towards the back of the room and are staring at us, waiting for her to come in and get things started. I look from them back to her, and she silently smiles as she waits for my answer. The sparkle in her eye is starting to fade as she realizes that I'm wasting her time, and all of theirs. The bitchy girl from last week who gave me and Em shit for talking makes a beeline for the stereo as soon as she realizes the instructor is here and gets the music blaring.

So what's it going to be?

"Not today, no. I was just walking by and wanted to see if my friend was here. Have a good workout!" Her face drops for a split second but instantly regains its natural smile as she becomes aware of her mistake. She cheerily repeats the gym standard "have a good workout," and before I know it she's bounced past me and up to the front of the class. As I turn to leave I swear I hear one of the girls at the back of the class snicker. She probably heard what I said about walking by ... good job, Charlie. It'll definitely be fun coming back here with Em and facing all of these girls. And don't forget the instructor!

@ @ @

I find Patrick standing in the entranceway as I open the front door. He gives me just enough room to take my shoes off and hang my keys up. He asks why I'm home so early in an accusatory tone; as if I'm not allowed to be home this early; as if I'd done something horribly wrong.

"Spin was cancelled so I just did a quick workout then left." I try to move past him into the hallway, but he won't budge. "Excuse me." Nothing. I try to push him out of my way, but he stubbornly refuses to move, keeping his arms crossed and his legs firmly planted. This is what I get for marrying someone who works out five times a week and recently joined the football league his office belongs to. The idea of lawyers playing on a football team together, and against other law offices, kills me. I back up and contemplate going out and running around to the back door to see if it's unlocked. It's very tempting. I don't doubt, however, that Patrick would instantly recognize my plan and simply repeat this move at the back door. I guess I don't have a choice.

When I finally stop trying to push past him he speaks. “I’m not going anywhere until you tell me that we’re going to talk about this. It’s been three days, Charlie. How long are you going to punish me for what I said?” His voice is filled with pain and his eyes with despair.

“You thought that I was trying to punish you? Seriously? That was the furthest thing from my mind. I just — I just can’t talk to you.” How can I explain this in a way that won’t hurt him any further? How can I make him understand?

“Charlie, come on. Why not? Please talk to me. You can’t just shut down and block me out like this; it isn’t fair. You’ve never done this before; I don’t know what I’m supposed to do.” His voice cracks with the last question, and so do I.

“I’m sorry, I wasn’t thinking of what this would be like for you. But you’re right; we should talk about this — we need to talk about this.” He finally lets me walk past him and into the house; he tries to pull me into the living room, but relents when I explain that I just need a few minutes to get settled and my head straight. I move around the house putting everything from my work and gym bags into its proper place: the manuscripts I just got today go in our shared office along with my laptop; the tea I picked up for Patrick from Starbucks goes in the kitchen pantry with the rest of our ever-growing collection; my unused gym clothes go back in their proper drawers in my dresser. When I finally finish putting everything away and change into comfier clothes I come downstairs to find Patrick on the couch waiting for me with my favourite almond tea.

◎ ◎ ◎

“Hi, Charlie? Dr. McLeod will see you now.” I get up and follow the receptionist down the short hall to my psychiatrist’s office even though this isn’t my first time here. The patients are never left alone in the office — there isn’t even a bathroom for us to use — we're either under the gaze of the receptionist, Anna, or that of the psychiatrist. I guess they don't trust us, and I'm not sure I blame them. The first time I came here a man was whispering that the devil set his brain on fire and that we should all be on the lookout for Satan's minions as they will try to take over our minds. The second time I came I met a woman who had cut open her neck because she thought it was the only sure-fire way to commit suicide; she made a joke about having two smiles that gave me nightmares for a week. At the end of my last appointment Dr. McLeod apologized; he explained that both patients I met were more "extreme" cases and couldn't always be trusted to leave when they were told to. Apparently we're not supposed to interact with other patients, let alone meet them, but I guess you can't always contain the crazy.

There are only two chairs in Dr. McLeod's office, and I head straight to the comfy brown leather one that I've sat in every visit thus far. Each time I've come in he's been standing, which I think is so I can choose which seat I'd prefer because he always sits immediately after I've made my decision. I can't help but wonder what he would say or do if I suddenly chose the other one. I've been trying to decide if he wants me to stay in the same chair or what, but I haven't figured it out yet so I stick with the brown leather one.

Apart from the chairs his office, which has to be at least three times the size of mine, has barely any furniture. Between us sits a small coffee table already set with tea for both of us, along with various pads of paper and pencils. During my first visit he asked me to draw how my anxiety makes me feel versus how the pregnancy makes me feel; one was in black and was a mess of spiralling scribbles and lines — the other was a heart within a sun with a question mark beside it, all in colour. In front of us is his enormous wooden desk covered with pens, papers, and personal items, each placed with precise care and forethought. I've also noticed a small silver frame on his desk that is alternately laid flat or propped up — I think depending on who he sees before me. Aside from that the only other pieces of furniture are the bookshelves that line the walls — all of the walls. If it wasn't my psychiatrist's office it would actually be my ideal library: a cozy place to hide away and read the stack of manuscripts that have been slowly accumulating on my desk.

"Good morning, Charlie, how have you been since our last appointment? Have things improved since your initial talk with Patrick?" He pauses to gauge my expression and continues when I nod in the affirmative. "We haven't really had time to talk about how things are between you and Patrick; I've been so focused on how you're coping with pregnancy and coming off your antidepressants because of it."

Ah yes, my Cipralex: that tiny white pill that has kept me sane these past five years. "Sane" being a relative term. The "fun" part has been freaking out about the possibility of more freak-outs. The week before I had become so anxious thinking that I wasn't going to be able to choose what to order when I went out for supper with Emily, Eric, and Patrick that I spent my entire lunch break looking at the menu for the restaurant we were going to that night. When Em called later that day to say that they wanted to go somewhere else, after I had finally made my decision, I apologized and said that I was feeling nauseous and had to reschedule. She was extremely understanding and told me not to worry; it wasn't a problem at all. I immediately called Patrick at work and told him the same thing. I came home to chicken noodle soup, dry toast, and a very attentive husband who hoped that the classic "sick-time" foods would also help with the nausea of pregnancy. He had even stopped on his way home to pick me up some ginger ale and stirred it to make it flat like my mom used to when I was a kid.

Dr. McLeod quietly clears his throat and snaps me back to reality.

"Well, like I mentioned before, it went better than I expected. He apologized for the trillionth time and tried to explain where he was coming from. I was happy to hear that he realized it was the wrong thing to say and definitely the wrong time to say it. I honestly don't think I've ever seen him so upset about something ... which was kind of nice to see." Dr. McLeod raises an eyebrow and jots something down in his notebook. Last visit I noticed that the bottom half of one bookcase is filled with notebooks: all different sizes and colours, and all with numbers on them; patient numbers, I assume. I find the anonymity comforting. I wait till he's finished writing whatever it might be, and continue.

"That sounds bad," I pause again, trying to accurately describe what I'm thinking, "it's just — it's nice to see that he genuinely feels bad for what he said and understands why it hurt me so much." I stop again, contemplating the gravity of what I'm about to say. "I honestly don't think I'll ever really forget what he said; I mean, I've forgiven him, and we've talked about it more since so I feel a lot better about all of it ... it's just..."

I stare down at my hands, not wanting to continue what I've begun saying. Dr. McLeod indulges my silence for a few minutes before coaxing me to say more.

"Just what, Charlie?"

I sigh. "It's stupid, but it's not the story I wanted for us."

"Story? What do you mean by that?" He drops his pen and notebook in his lap; Dr. McLeod genuinely seems interested. Despite the fact that I know he's getting paid a lot of good money to sit here and listen to me babble on, I appreciate the fact that he legitimately cares about what I say and what I think. It helps being able to talk to someone so completely removed from the rest of my life and all of its problems. It also helps that I feel like one of his "saner" patients; I feel comfortable knowing I look absolutely normal in comparison. It's horrible, but true.

"Well, just that when we tell the story about how I found out I was pregnant I don't exactly want to tell the truth." I look down at my hands again, embarrassed to be admitting this.

"Why? Are you concerned what people will think about it?" *Well, duh. Anyone who hears what happened will instantly know that I'm carrying a baby that my husband doesn't want.* No one will think that. *I think that.* I think a lot of things; that doesn't make them true. *If this one isn't true why am I so upset about it?* Because I can't trust myself enough to know either way.

"Yes, I am. But I don't think that's irrational ... it was a shitty situation and neither of us comes off well."

"But it was real. When my brother-in-law found out that my sister was having twins he fainted and smacked his head on the counter on the way down. He needed several stitches." Dr. McLeod smacks his forehead with his palm as he says this and we both laugh. "He was extremely embarrassed at the time, but he can now look back on it and laugh. And it doesn't mean he loves his kids any less. It's just what happened; he couldn't control it. Neither can you. And neither can Patrick."

"I understand what you're saying, I really do. And while I can recognize that you're right, it doesn't change how horrible I feel right now. It sucks."

"Oh, I don't disagree with you there. I just want you to focus on why it bothers you – not why it would bother other people. I know that's hard, especially given the type of anxiety disorder that you have." I cringe when he says this. "But for the sake of this baby, and for your own mental well-being, you need to remember that at the end of the day what other people may think or say about you does not determine your own happiness or reality. No one in this world, other than you and Patrick, know what your relationship looks like from the inside; focus on the two of you, and the little one on the way." He looks down at his notebook as if remembering something, and I quickly wipe the tears from my eyes. Patrick would like Dr. McLeod and what he just said; he's very adamant about the fact that when it comes to us and our relationship we shouldn't care what other people think. And for the most part I don't; it's just sometimes... Sometimes you can't control what you think. Or what you feel. Dr. McLeod taps his notebook and resumes talking. "I'm sorry, though, I took us away from my original question; not that I think that wasn't an important and helpful tangent."

My mind has completely wandered off topic so it takes me a minute to get reoriented.

"Oh, yeah. Once he apologized and tried to explain his behaviour he told me that he is fully behind us having this baby."

"And do you believe him?" That's the question I've been asking myself since he said it. Over, and over, and over again.

"Honestly? I don't know. I want to — I really, really want to. But I just don't know... He couldn't even make it to the first ultrasound appointment because he said he couldn't get the time off work, and I get that but still...

"I know it sounds stupid, but I just have a feeling that this isn't what he wants; that he's just going through the motions because he knows I want this. And it scares me because we have six-and-a-half more months of this and I don't know how he's going to react when my belly starts getting bigger and the reality of what's happening hits him harder." Or when he feels it kick for the first time. Or when I begin buying the crib, the car seat, and the millions of other things that we'll need.

"Since his initial reaction has he given you any sort of physical proof that he doesn't want this child? Has he said or done anything specifically that raises some flags? I do not want to devalue what you are feeling, but I want to make sure that it is grounded in fact. Normally I would shy away from being so blunt, but I think it might help you: using your own words, are you sure that this isn't all in your head? That you haven't created this problem?" His voice softens as he says this, as if to temper the blow of his words.

"I don't know. I might have? Maybe I'm just projecting my own fears onto Patrick and imagining things that aren't there. I've been trying to figure that out and I haven't really gotten anywhere. Being off the Cipralex ... it kind of makes it harder to distinguish between my anxious thinking and normal thinking. If that makes sense?

"Whenever I try to talk about the pregnancy he just smiles and nods or he'll just get up and say that he has a case that he needs to work on... But I don't know if that's because he's busy with work or because he doesn't want to talk about this." And I don't know if I'm freaking out because I genuinely think he doesn't want the baby or because I'm being irrational. The mental backflips are exhausting.

"As difficult as I know this will be," Dr. McLeod says, "I think that you really need to try and forget his initial reaction; it's negatively affecting how you see him and his behaviour now. Don't worry about what he's going to be like when you find out the sex of the baby or when he feels the first kick, something that freaks any man out, and just focus on now. Take it day by day." He looks me straight in the eye as he asks the next question. "Do you trust him?"

"Of course." I don't even have to think; it's an automatic response.

"Then trust that he's telling you the truth." The alarm on his desk goes off and we both stand. "Unfortunately that's all for today. Anna should have your next appointment scheduled but double-check with her before you leave. I look forward to our next visit."

"Me too." Despite my initial apprehension of seeing a psychiatrist, and the fear of opening up to some complete stranger about how crazy I find myself at times, I genuinely like meeting with Dr. McLeod. I don't know if it's actually helping, but it feels like it is, which actually means a hell of a lot more.

@ @ @

Walking downstairs to the exit on the main floor I'm delighted to find that the gloomy fog that had been rising when I entered the building is gone, and has been replaced by a wonderfully shining sun. I tilt my head upwards as I step outside to feel the warmth of its rays, and almost trip down the stairs. Luckily no one sees, and I manage a quick recovery. I wish I could stay fixed in this spot for the rest of the day, turning ever so slightly as the sun moves across the sky, but Patrick is waiting and I don't want to make him sit in a hot car any longer than he has to. I force myself to turn away from the sun and towards the parking lot where I see our SUV sitting in the shade. Guess I could've made him wait a little longer after all.

"What are these?" I ask Patrick as I climb into the passenger seat beside him. There are three small presents sitting on my seat, and I can tell they're from him because it looks like a child wrapped them. I have to hide the smile on my face; he hates it when I make fun of his wrap jobs. We bug each other a lot but for some reason that one really seems to bother him. The man is great at many things but somehow never learnt how to use wrapping paper and tape. Since we've gotten married I've taken over all of the present wrapping, not that I'm complaining — I find it oddly relaxing and enjoyable. There's just something so fulfilling about a beautifully wrapped present, especially when the folds are clean and precise and the bow matches the paper perfectly.

Patrick's face is a mixture of expectancy and apprehension, and he waits till I'm buckled up and comfortable before he speaks.

"Just a little something for my favourite momma-to-be. I know that when you first met with Dr. McLeod you were a little nervous, and while it sounds like it's going well I thought it'd be nice to have a surprise for you when you got out." He hasn't started the car yet, despite my seatbelt being on, and is instead intently staring at the gifts on my lap. I think he's more excited about me opening them than I am by the way he's fidgeting in his seat and playing with the keys.

"Well, that's very thoughtful. Does that mean I get a surprise every time I come here?" I look over at him as sweetly as I can, trying not to laugh. Patrick fakes a shocked expression, as if I have just suggested something horrible.

"Depends on how often you plan on seeing this guy," he says and we both laugh. "They're surprises, so you're just going to have to wait and see! How did it go today though?" And with that small question his voice changes, losing its upbeat tone. There's a lot I haven't told him about my experiences with anxiety so I'm sure he can't help but wonder what Dr. McLeod and I talk about. He would be devastated if he heard the conversations that focused on him.

"Do you think that going to him will help with ... all of this?" It kills me to see the pain hidden behind his smile, questioning why he isn't enough; why I need someone else to help me.

"I do — I..." The tears begin quietly falling down my cheeks as I read the inscription that he has written on the inside cover of *What to Expect When You're Expecting*, the first present I have opened. The first gift I've received as an expectant mother. Printed neatly, in the nicest writing I have ever seen of his, is a page-long inscription on the opening flap. I have to hold the book up in front of me to prevent the tears from hitting the page and making the ink bleed.

Charlie,

I can't imagine how scared and anxious you must be feeling right now — I wish I could so that I would know exactly what to do and say to help you. I promise to do whatever I can over the next six-and-a-half months, and many, many years to come, to make sure that whatever you are feeling, you don't have to suffer through it alone. I promise to be here for you and this baby no matter what, and I promise to love both of you with all that I have. While there will be a lot of things we cannot control throughout this pregnancy, I wanted to get you this book (a bit of a cliché, I know) to help explain anything you may be feeling or experiencing because of the pregnancy. I may not be able to fully help you deal with your anxiety, but I will learn as much as I can about pregnancy and babies so that the changes you go through will stress you out as little as possible. You are an incredible woman and I know that you can do this. And whenever you feel like you can't — like everything is weighing you down and you don't see any hope in sight — I will be here to support you and help you. Even when I don't know what to say, even if that just means holding you or making you laugh. You are going to be an amazing mother, never doubt that.

I love you and that little peanut of ours.

Love forever and always,

Patrick.

"Charlie, are you okay?" The quiet tears have built into a sob by the time I finish reading the inscription. I'm shaking uncontrollably, letting out everything that I have been desperately trying to hold in.

"This — I — You — I..." I can barely get anything out in between sobs. I'm ugly-crying now, but it won't stop. The only response I can make is to shake my head "yes." I can see his body relax. I give myself a few minutes to calm down before trying to speak again, knowing that if I try too soon it will only bring on another wave of crying. "Thank you, this is — this means so much to me. You mean so much to me, and I couldn't do this without you. I've been so scared that you're still having a difficult time accepting this. So reading this? It means ... everything. I know it bothers you that I need to see a psychiatrist, it's just that—"

"No, Charlie, please don't think that. It's not that I'm bothered by it; it's just ... I just feel useless sometimes, like I should be able to help you but I can't. I know there are times, even in the past, when something has been bothering you, but you won't talk about it with me. And I don't want to force you to talk about things with me if you don't want to ... so I don't push." I hear the sadness creep into his voice and I begin crying again. I've hurt the man I love without even realizing it. *Am I always this oblivious to the effects of my actions? How many times have I unknowingly hurt him?*

"It's never that I don't want to talk to you about something. It's just ... I don't want to burden you with my problems. The majority of the things I get upset about are all in my head — they're things I've created in my own mind — and they rarely have anything to do with anything that you, or anyone else for that matter, have done or said. I don't like talking about it because I know it's all in my head; they're my own problems to deal with.

"But I don't want you to ever think you aren't enough for me or that I don't want you to help me. Because that has never been the case. There is no one in the world who I trust more than you or who I feel more comfortable with. You've seen my crazy more than anyone else has because I know you can handle it and I don't want to hide things from you. It's just ... I need to talk to the psychiatrist because he's completely removed from my world – he can view my life and anxiety impartially. This is what he does for a living – helping people – and there are just some burdens that I can't ask you to carry. I know that you would, but I just can't."

The car is quiet for a few minutes as both of us sit there letting my words seep in. I hope he understands what I'm trying to say, because I honestly can't think of another way to say it. I don't know how to explain the fact that there are just some things about myself that I can't let him see or know. *It would kill me for him to see just how broken and crazy I am. I know he loves me, but ... I don't know if he would still love me if I let him see everything, if I showed him just how fucked up I am. I've shown him more than anyone else I have ever known, but I just can't. I can't risk it. I don't like this side of myself so how could I expect him to?* There are some thoughts and feelings that are better left unsaid.

We pull up to the house with the remaining presents still unopened on my lap. The only sounds are the closing of the car doors and the jingling of the keys as Patrick lets us inside the house. *Did I say something wrong? Did I make things worse?* The silence is closing in on me. Suffocating me. I'm about to say something to break the silence when he pulls me in for a hug; I let the presents fall to the floor as I wrap my arms around him, burying my face in his neck. I breathe in deeply, instantly calmed by his embrace and the comforting combination of his deodorant, body wash, and cologne. He makes fun of me when I say that he smells good, but there's just something about him that smells like home.

“I hope none of that was breakable,” I whisper. He quietly laughs.

“No, we’re all good.” But he’s not just talking about the presents anymore. “I know I freaked you out really badly about not wanting this baby, but I promise to do whatever I can to show you that I do want it.” With that he picks me up and carries me to the couch, throwing me onto it before going to grab the rest of the presents that I dropped.

What if he’s just doing all of this because he knows it’s what I want? What if he’s just going through the motions? What if — oh god — what if when he holds our baby he feels nothing for it? What if he hates it, or me? Will I ever truly know if he wants this? Will I ever believe him?

@ @ @

A few stormy weeks later we leave for Winnipeg, our first visit home since we’ve moved. Despite everything, we decide to still go. We’ve been planning the mini road trip for some time. It’s the longest Patrick’s mom has gone without seeing him; she’s beyond excited. Things between the two of us have been rocky for the past few days, but I hope that it won’t continue into the trip. Unfortunately the drive is worse than I expected: nothing but yelling. Well, maybe not all of it is spent yelling — but it feels like it. An hour in, Patrick springs the fact that he doesn’t want to tell his parents about the baby yet; his argument is that the first trimester is when I’m most likely to miscarry. I’m shocked that of all the topics he could have brought up to start talking about my pregnancy, this is the one he chose. I ask if that is what he wants to happen, and of course he says no, that it would be a horrible thing to happen to me; he says nothing of how heartbreaking it would be to lose the baby. I clutch my stomach the entire time feeling the need to protect the growing life inside of me at whatever cost.

The only time we stop arguing is when we stop for gas or food. I don't think either of us wants to make a scene in front of a handful of strangers. Instead we make small talk and pick out snacks from the gas station like everything is fine; we are the perfect loving couple. It is exhausting and I'm relieved to sneak off to the bathroom and have a few moments of peace to myself. As soon as we get back into the car the fighting resumes; it seems like whatever one of us says angers or upsets the other. Nothing is right. No one can win.

He's livid when I finally tell him that I've already shared the news with my parents and Emily; I was too excited and I couldn't wait. I've never seen him so angry before. He starts yelling at me, telling me that I had no right to do that — that I shouldn't have done that. I ask him why over and over again, trying to understand, but he refuses to explain himself. He won't even listen when I tell him that it isn't fair, that I need someone to share in my happiness because he refuses to. He brings up the presents he gave me outside of Dr. McLeod's office, and I counter that that was the only time he willingly spoke of my being pregnant. He becomes silent when I hint that the presents were merely a ploy to get me off his back; that he was just doing what he thought I wanted. He doesn't understand that I just want him to be honest — to tell me the truth, regardless of what it may be.

Blinded by my anger, I finally bring up what he said when he came home drunk the night we found out I was pregnant; he denies any remembrance of it, and I argue that he wouldn't have said it if he didn't mean it, no matter how drunk he was. I never wanted to bring it up; I wanted to forget that it had ever happened. I'd been trying to follow Dr. McLeod's advice and focus on how Patrick has been since, but I can't stop the nagging voice that tells me he was just trying to cover up how he truly felt. I'm left not knowing which Patrick to believe. Then of course I start crying as I ask him, for what feels like the thousandth time, if he really wants this baby or not. Instead of his usual automatic response, "of course," I'm met with silence. For the first time during the drive he says nothing. Both hands are on the steering wheel, and he stares straight ahead at the road while I plead with him to answer me — to tell me the truth. Without taking his eyes off the road he quietly says, "I don't know," and I feel my world slowly crumbling beneath me. I ask him about the many conversations we had before we got married about having kids; how during them he had excitedly talked about the Halloween costumes he would dress them in. He always said that he wanted to have two or three. His only response is, "I thought I did." Neither of us says a word after that for the rest of the drive. It's a long three hours.

@ @ @

You'd think it's been years instead of a few months by the number of questions and hugs we get as we walk in the door. Patrick and his mom talk weekly on the phone, and she's always texting me, but that's not enough for her. It's not that I don't like her; we get along fantastically and I love spending time with his family. It's just that she can be a touch too much. Patrick calls it overbearing. Sometimes I pretend to be out of the house and hide out in the basement when she calls, but one time I stayed down there for over an hour. Patrick was not happy when he found me, but luckily since we were in the basement I don't think the neighbours heard the yelling. Since then I've tried to be more understanding and available. The more I talk to her on the phone the less he has to.

For our first night back in the Peg, Patrick's mom goes all out for supper; within half an hour of our arrival the table is set and filled. The table's so crowded with all of

Patrick's favourites that there's barely enough room to hold all six place settings. Not that I'm complaining; while I love to cook, my meals cannot compare to his mom's. Tonight she has made: Red Lobster buns, of which I have four even though they're the size of my hand; pasta with both Alfredo sauce and his nana's red sauce; Caesar salad; and chicken parmesan. And once supper's done and she's finished haranguing us about eating more because she's made oh-so-much, I know she'll pull out whatever dessert Patrick's sister's made. To top it off, there's the pile of alcohol his dad pulls out of the liquor cabinet for us. After refusing a drink several times I can't help but wonder if his parents are getting suspicious. This is probably the first time I haven't accepted a drink from their ever-stocked supply of liquor and wine — it pays to like the same wine as your mother-in-law.

And then I tell them. And suddenly the family is staring at me with giant smiles plastered on each and every one of their faces. Except Patrick's, which shows a mixture of shock and horror as I continue speaking. Luckily all eyes are on me; they can't see his eyes narrow in anger, or how the colour drains from his face before it turns a bright shade of red. Before I can even tell them how far along I am, his mom pulls me out of my chair to give me a hug, and his dad, sister, and brother-in-law follow her lead. Patrick says nothing; the shock won't allow him to. Not that they've even noticed; they're all busy talking over each other about how happy they are for us and how excited they are to be a nana, a papa, an aunt, and an uncle. Patrick just stands there, watching this all unfold around him. He tries to sit back down, but a fresh round of hugs prevents him from doing so: their joy is endless. He remains silent for the rest of the evening, and when one of his family members brings up the pregnancy or asks him about it Patrick just smiles and nods at whatever they're saying. He doesn't say a word to me.

We slowly walk up the stairs to his old bedroom, silently passing hallway photos depicting years of family vacations and holidays. They span decades of Patrick's life, culminating with a picture of the two of us from our wedding. I can't help but think about having a family picture of us up there: me, Patrick, and our little one. I start thinking about who our baby will look like: whose eyes they'll have, what colour their hair will be, even the shape of their nose. This image is quickly erased as Patrick bolts straight past me and into the bathroom, making sure to avoid all contact. The "click" of the lock punctuates the silence between us. I softly rap at the door but he turns the water on full blast, effectively blocking me out. I knock a few more times then give up. When Patrick finally turns off the water, I speak.

"Patrick, please, don't do this — don't shut me out like this. We need to talk about what happened, what's happening right now, because you're scaring me." *Scaring me? I'm absolutely fucking terrified of what's going on... I'm the one who runs and hides, not him*. Patrick opens the door as quickly and as quietly as he possibly can; his eyes meet mine and he quickly pulls me into the bathroom with him. I reach out to him, try to touch his arm, but he flinches and recoils from my touch. I feel nauseous — as if I've received a blow to the stomach; the weight of his reaction forces me to take a step back. "Patrick — please..."

"Enough." He says this so harshly that I immediately stop, biting my closed lips for fear of saying something, of pushing him further than I already have. "I've been trying to be good about this. I really have. I've tried to be supportive and excited and happy and everything that an expectant parent is supposed to be," his whole demeanour changes: his shoulders slump, his head drops, and the light fades from his eyes. "But I'm exhausted. And then without any warning you tell my entire family about what's going on—"

"What's going on? Are you fucking serious right now? It's called being pregnant, you jackass; it's called having a baby." With my arms wrapped tightly around my belly I back up until I hit the door then lean into it.

"Jesus Christ, Charlie, can you please just shut up." A look of sadness flickers across his eyes but is gone by the time his hand is clamped over my mouth to silence my words before they can jump out. If Patrick sees the pain in my eyes he ignores it. "You know I didn't want to tell my parents yet — you knew that — and yet you went completely against everything I said and told them! We talked about this on the fucking drive here, there's no way you forgot. And yet you tell them the first night that we're here, and of course you didn't give me any warning, you just couldn't do what I wanted, could you? Why? Why, Charlie, can you not just think about what I want for once? What was I supposed to do, Charlie, hmm? I don't want to lie to my parents ... but I can't exactly tell them the truth either..." *What.* What.

I rip his hand away, dropping it from my face. "What? ... What do you mean you can't tell them the truth...?"

"You heard me. And you know exactly what I'm talking about." *Of course I do. Denying what's happening isn't making it go away — I can't keep pretending that everything's okay — clearly neither of us can.*

"I do." Defeated, I lean in to give him a goodnight kiss but miss when he backs away. "I don't know what you want me to do, Patrick. I give up." I walk away and I'm asleep before he comes to bed.

@ @ @

The next morning Patrick's parents are out and he tries to talk to me again about what happened while we have breakfast. His mom has left us two plates of food in the fridge, each with bacon, pancakes, and hash browns; she's also left a big bowl of fruit salad for us to share. It's not surprising that Patrick's dad has put on a few pounds in his retirement. What is surprising, though, is Patrick's behaviour. Normally he's the calm, rational one in our relationship, and gets over things rather quickly. But this time his anger, if anything, has only intensified from the night before, but instead of being loud and vocal, he's seething with a quiet rage. It terrifies me. He begins asking me things that will haunt me for the rest of my life: the worst question he asks is what we would do if he decided he doesn't want to be a father. And I can't take it. I've been asking myself the same question since the night we found out that I'm pregnant. It's too much for me to bear listening to him vocalize my fear; to finally put into words what his actions have been saying all along. A sudden wave of overwhelming sadness hits me and I begin to cry.

"Oh god, what is it now?" I look up at him and see the tired look on his face; the look that says he's sick of all of this. Of me.

"It's nothing." And as I say this I can feel a tightening within my stomach that slowly begins to spread to my chest. My body is trying to pull inwards, and everything begins to tense. I move to stand, but my whole body begins to feel as if it's shutting down: a tingling sensation travels out from my stomach to my arms and legs, slowly making its way to my hands and feet. Every inch of my body experiences the unnerving feeling of pins and needles all at once; no part of me can escape it. I begin shaking and my eyes widen. Something is very, very wrong. And I start crying; it's the only thing I can do at this point. I am absolutely terrified because I have never felt anything like this before; I've lost all control of my body and I have no idea why.

"Charlie, what's wrong? Is it the baby? What's happening?" Each question he asks me is filled with more panic than the last. When I don't answer right away he repeats each question with greater urgency. I feel my hands contracting and pulling into themselves. I fall to the floor as my legs stop supporting my weight. I try to protect my stomach as I fall, but my arms and hands are completely useless. There's nothing I can do. I begin to cry even harder but manage to get out, "Call an ambulance," before the tingling sensation spreads to my face, and my mouth is no longer able to form words. My eyes begin to close, and the last image I see is Patrick frantically running to his phone. Something has taken over my body.

"Ambulance," he says.

"It's my wife. I don't know. One minute we were talking and the next... She's pregnant. Twelve weeks.

"I don't know. Her eyes are closed and her hands are clenched. No, I don't think she can stand. Let me check.

"Charlie? Charlie, can you hear me?"

The tears haven't stopped flowing from my eyes despite their being closed, but I nod my head as much as my tensed neck and shoulders allow: "yes."

"Oh, thank god. Yes, yes, she can hear me. No, she just nodded her head.

"137 Burrows Avenue. Thank you, and please – please hurry."

I can't help but be amazed at how calm Patrick sounded while talking to the 9-1-1 operator. As soon as he hangs up I can feel him gently lift my body against his and carry me to the front door, going as slowly as he possibly can to make sure he doesn't hurt me.

"I've got you. I've got you, Charlie. And ... and our little peanut." He barely makes it to the door before he starts crying. I can feel the tears drop against my face and mix with my own. I wish I could comfort him and tell him that I'm okay, that the baby's okay. But I can't. Not just because I can't speak, but because I don't know.

What if I'm losing the baby? *Oh god. What if this is some form of premature labour?* This doesn't make sense; I'm not having any contractions. *My hands...* My hands don't count. Don't be stupid, Charlie. I'm not going into labour. *Then what the fuck is happening to me?! What's going on? Why can't I talk? I can't even use my hands they're so tightly clenched. I can't walk. And my entire body feels all tingly like a foot does before it falls asleep. Before it goes numb. Oh god, fuck. It's already happening. My legs are going numb. Holy shit. What if this happens to my entire body? What is happening inside my body? WHAT IF THIS HURTS THE BABY?! Oh god. Oh god. What the fuck is happening to me?*

Suddenly I hear sirens nearing the house; for how long Patrick's been listening for them I don't know. A cool breeze hits my face as Patrick flings the door open to let the paramedics in. Well at least I can still feel that...

"She's right here. Please be careful." I think he's stopped crying, but I can still hear his voice catch when he speaks. Of course I've been too self-absorbed to consider how terrifying this must be for him. I don't know what's going on inside my own body, but at least I can feel that something's wrong. He has absolutely no idea what's happening to me or our baby.

"Sir, can you please let go of her?" I can feel the paramedic try to pry Patrick's hands off of my arms. But I don't want him to. I can't see Patrick, but at least feeling him is something. I can hear the paramedics talking to each other as they carry me to the ambulance on a stretcher, but I don't know what they're saying. I'm too busy listening for Patrick. I need to hear him; to know where he is. But if he's making any noise I can't hear it. And I feel so alone.

As they lift me into the back of the ambulance I hear one of the men talking to Patrick.

"You can come in the back with her, sir. Just make sure to stay out of the way."

"Can I — can I hold her hand?" The paramedic must be able to hear the desperation in Patrick's voice as clearly as I do because his voice softens the next time he speaks.

"Yes that's fine, but only after I'm done checking her vitals because I'll need to attach the cardiac monitor and oximeter to her arms, chest, and hands. But once I'm done then you're more than welcome to."

"Thank you."

The door slams shut and I hear the sirens turn on. Everyone is talking over me and around me, but I shut them out. Instead I focus on trying to open my eyes, to move my hand. Something to let Patrick know that I'm okay, that I'm still here. *But what if I'm not? What if there are problems with the baby, things that I have caused, that can't be shown with these tests? What if I've done permanent damage that won't be realized until it's older?* Sometimes the most disruptive problems can't be seen, only felt. *What if its mind is like mine...? What if, despite everything that Patrick and I do or say, it ends up like me?*

All of a sudden the back of the ambulance goes silent. All I can hear are the machines working around me and the sirens demanding that people move out of our way; neither the paramedic nor Patrick makes a sound. Slowly I feel warmth building between my legs; oh god, did I seriously just pee myself? Well, that's horribly embarrassing — but maybe with the blanket over top of me they won't be able to tell?

The silence is broken when I hear Patrick whisper, "Is that blood?" And while I can't see anything I imagine that the paramedic nods his head "yes," because the next thing I know Patrick has broken down. I've never heard him like this before; the crying has taken on an almost animalistic quality that the ambulance can barely contain. I try to open my eyes to see him, but I can't; the most I can do is turn my head towards him.

@ @ @

Four hours and a dozen tests later we're both sitting on my hospital bed together, holding on to each other for dear life.

They said that I had an anxiety attack.

I've never had one before.

They said it caused added stress both on my heart and the baby's.

They said her little heart couldn't take it.

They said I lost her.

They didn't have to say it but I know.

Patrick knows.

I can see it in the way he looks at me.

The way they all look at me.

I did this.

He tries to hide how he truly feels; I know better.

He's relieved.

Acknowledgements

There are so many people I have to thank for helping make this novella possible — from former professors and teachers, to the dozens of people who donated to my crowdfunding campaign — this book would not have been possible without all of you.

To my Mom: thank you for always supporting me and believing in me — I would not be where I am today without your love and guidance, and I would not be half as strong and independent as I am now. Thank you for always being my biggest supporter, my loudest fan, and the best mom that I could have ever asked for.

And of course, thank you to every single person that contributed to my crowdfunding page! Without all of your generous donations this book would not have been possible - thank you, everyone, for helping my dream come true. A special thank-you goes out to the people, listed below, who donated the most sizeable contributions to my crowdfunding:

Richard Almond
Wendy & Bruce Astle
Carol & Andrew Brigham
Paula & Denis Bentz
Taina Chahal
Paul Charrette
Rob Deleo
Cathy Ebenhoeh
Jenna Grace
Michele & Wes Grace
Adam Gustafson
Anna Guttman
Angela Gysen
Sue & Stan Koch
Sharon Kozak
Ron Marostica
Robert Mazur
Sean & Sara McFarlane
Thomas Mueller
Leah Nadin
Jack & Diane Playford
John Playford
Scott Pound
Mark Rauch
Jodey Rowlandson
Dawn Schaller
Diane Schaller
Ken Schaller
Fred & Helen Schaller
Teresa Socha
Janet Verge
Jan & Rob Whybourne
Jan Wieckowski
Cassandra Woit

www.ingramcontent.com/pod-product-compliance
Ingram Content Group UK Ltd.
Pitfield, Milton Keynes, MK11 3LW, UK
UKHW041632190726
13854UKWH00006B/2457

9 781771 801737